Amber Waiting

Nan Gregory
Illustrated by Kady MacDonald Denton

Red Deer Press

Here's something good about kindergarten. Getting a turn on the swing. Amber swings high. Her toes reach for the roof of the school. She's almost flying.

Here's another good thing. Painting. The brushes are fat. The colours are bright. Amber wears her dad's shirt to keep herself clean. She and her classmates paint a lovely garden for the hall.

More good things. Picture books of faraway places. Amber is gentle with the pages. Tying her shoes. Her teacher tells her, "Make two bunny ears." Amber can do it! And in the snow, bundling up and sliding around.

Here's the bad thing about kindergarten. Waiting for Dad.

Amber's dad is late again.

Amber sits in the hallway and waits. Her coat is neatly buttoned. Her laces are handily tied. She's right ready to go.

Her classmates have long since hurried up home.
Lunchtime rings loud over her head. Big kids swarm up and
down the corridor. Teachers swish in and out of the office.

Today is bake sale day. The secretary buys her a treat.
Amber chooses the muffin with the bluest icing and the
rainbow sprinkles. She crunches the sprinkles between her
teeth and watches the hands click, tick, click around the
big, dull face of the clock. The halls fall quiet. Amber
sings a little made-up song for company.

Amber can paint pretty flowers. She's fearless on the swings. She can slide without falling when puddles are icy. She ties her own shoes. She's learning to read.

Where's her dad?

Waiting so long every day gives Amber time to plan. One day she'll find out how to fly, and when she does, she'll pick up her dad and fly him away to the moon. She'll tell him, "I'll be back in no time."

Then she'll swing high in cold places with penguins and hot places where elephants are. Her feet will touch rooftops! Dads all over the world will see.

She'll paint pictures of pansy faces and tulip heads, and hang them on shoe laces stretched between mountains. Dads will stop and marvel.

She'll sing her own tune with her own words, and a satellite will catch them and throw them back to all the TVs the dads are watching, and the dads will hear.

She'll whiz around on frozen rivers, and all
the dads will see the message her skates
make on the ice.

"That reminds me," the dads will say.
"Someone very important is waiting for me."

All this time her dad will be on the moon, watching the stars rush home and the sun come up with no hands on its face.

At last she'll go and get him. He'll be so glad to see her.
He'll understand about waiting.

Then, when kindergarten's out, Amber's dad will be there already. All the late dads all over the world will be there already. The late moms, too. They'll pick up their girls and their boys, lift them onto their shoulders, and ride them high home.

That would be the best thing about kindergarten.

At last, at last, here comes Amber's dad. Amber is on her feet, right ready to go.

"Do you realize what time it is?" says the secretary.

Amber's dad glances at the wall clock. "Whoops," he says and smiles his famous smile.

He swings the door open. "Let's go, sweetie."

Amber trots to keep up.

"Dad," she says, "were you ever on the moon?"

"On the moon?"

She tugs him to a stop. "Waiting for someone. Scared and lonely."

He frees his sleeve and starts away again.

Then something stills him.

"Oh," he says. His face falls quiet.

Amber waits.

"I see what you mean," he says.

Amber reaches out. "Carry me, Dad?"

"I sure will."

He gives her a kiss on the way up.

Then swings her onto his shoulders. Rides her high home.

Northern Lights Books for Children are published by
Red Deer Press
813 MacKimmie Library Tower
2500 University Drive N.W.
Calgary Alberta Canada T2N 1N4
www.reddeerpress.com

Credits
Edited for the Press by Peter Carver
Cover and text design by Blair Kerrigan/Glyphics
Printed and bound in Canada for Red Deer Press

Acknowledgments
Financial support provided by the Canada Council, the Department of Canadian Heritage, the Alberta Foundation for the Arts, a beneficiary of the Lottery Fund of the Government of Alberta, and the University of Calgary.

National Library of Canada Cataloguing in Publication Data
Gregory, Nan
Amber waiting
(Northern lights books for children)
ISBN 0-88995-258-2
I. Denton, Kady MacDonald. II. Title. III. Series.
PS8563.R4438A82 2002   jC813'.54   C2002-910847-0
PZ7.G86235Am 2002

5 4 3 2 1

For Sol, who waited.
— Nan Gregory

To my children who have often told me how long they waited.
— Kady MacDonald Denton